Ola's
Wake

Ola's Wake

BJ Stone

Henry Holt and Company * New York

With gratitude to my Tuesday critique group, who supported me and cheered me up when I was down.

Many thanks to my editor, Christy Ottaviano, who is always upbeat, and who taught me patience in the publishing process.

Henry Holt and Company, LLC
Publishers since 1866
115 West 18th Street, New York, New York 10011

Henry Holt is a registered trademark of Henry Holt and Company, LLC

Library of Congress Cataloging-in-Publication Data
Stone, BJ. Ola's wake / BJ Stone p.   cm.
Summary: Having traveled to the Ozark Mountains of Missouri to attend
great-grandmother Ola's funeral, ten-year-old Josie hears many colorful
stories about a strong and generous relative she does not remember.
[1. Great-grandmothers—Fiction. 2. Ozark Mountains—Fiction.
3. Mountain life—Missouri—Fiction. 4. Missouri—Fiction.]   I. Title.
PZ7.S875942 O1 2000   [Fic]—dc21   99-48325

ISBN 0-8050-6157-6
First Edition—2000
Printed in the United States of America on acid-free paper. ∞
1   3   5   7   9   10   8   6   4   2

In loving memory of my mother,
whose life inspired this book

Contents

Ola's
Wake

The Car Ride

If my great-grandmother Ola hadn't died, I might never have known her. The day we got the news, Ginny, that's what I call my mama, said we had to leave Texas and drive up to the Ozarks for her funeral. I didn't want to go. I didn't even know her Granny Ola.

Ginny put her hands on her hips and glared at me with her eyes, greener than lime sherbet. She pushed my legs off the arm of the chair, where I lay sprawled sketching scenes for her poems. Ginny makes extra money writing verse for a card publishing outfit when she's not working at the diner. I try to help, but now all she wanted from me was to get out of the chair, leave Texas, and go all the way to the Missouri Ozarks for a funeral.

"We have to go," she said. "Granny Ola doesn't have any family left, except maybe for a cousin of mine. Besides, I don't have anyone to leave you with." She put her arms around me and said, "Josephine, we're going to Granny Ola's funeral, and that's final."

Ginny usually calls me Josie, so when she used Josephine, I knew it was final, whether I liked it or not. But she was right. Since my dad ran out, I couldn't stay with him on account of no one knows where he is.

And I can't stay with Grandma Louise anymore. She died in a car wreck when I was seven. One minute she was here and the next gone. Ginny said I was too young to go to her funeral, so I stayed with a neighbor in the trailer park. This time I guess I don't have any choice but to go.

After dinner, we loaded our suitcases into Ginny's old fishtail Cadillac, the one Grandma Louise left her. Ginny said that her mama hardly ever drove the car, so it was in mint condition. I told her we ought to sell it and get a Bug, one that didn't guzzle so much gas. But Ginny wanted to keep it. "Anyway," she said, "we can't afford to buy a car, not even a VW."

I guess we're poor. Our trailer is the runt of the Garden Mobile Home Estates. Ginny says that we can hook up for less than we'd have to pay for an apartment. She thinks it's a lot safer for us and easier to move if she takes a mind to. We have friendly neighbors. Thing is, I'm the only kid. All my friends are older than Ginny, but I don't mind too much. They loan me books and play gin rummy with me whenever I want.

After we told the landlord where we were going and to please check our mail, we turned off our window cooler and headed east out of Fort Worth. It was a hot summer night and we about sweltered as we drove through the flat countryside toward McKinney.

I traced our trip on the road map for a while through onion and cotton farm country, until we drove into darkness with beaming headlights almost blinding us. We zoomed north up to Muskogee, Oklahoma, then over to Tahlequah. I remembered studying about the Cherokees, and figured these towns had Indian names.

Ginny started teaching me at home after we moved so many times trying to live close to her jobs. I told her I didn't want to go to another new school where I didn't know anybody. The last school I was in, Ginny would drop me off, and by the time she got home, I'd already run out of the building and headed for our trailer park. She finally got a few assignments with a card company, but she couldn't get any work done, as she was always trying to get me back in school. That's when she decided she'd teach me herself, even if she did have to dodge the truant officers.

We go to the library once a week and check out as many books as we can carry in an old canvas bag. She lets me get books I'm interested in, then she assigns stuff for me to do, like comparing climate and food of different places, or characters in novels. I have to write a lot, and it's hard work, but we can switch our subjects around whenever we want and even take trips to the park or museums without asking permission from anybody. That's how we became such good pals, almost like sisters. Only she's the boss.

Once we turned east out of Tahlequah, we got into hilly country. Ginny said that we would drive the whole four hundred fifty-something miles without stopping. In Arkansas, the blacktop road was lined with pine trees on each side, and the moon's bright face peeked through them. The trees zipped past so fast it made me dizzy.

Ginny gripped the steering wheel like maybe she could make the car go faster that way. She drank coffee from a thermos to stay awake, and listened to the radio play "Hang on Sloopy." Mostly that's what I was doing, hanging on. Sometimes I slept when I wasn't holding a flashlight and tracing the road on our map.

~~~

After driving all night, we headed north into the Missouri Ozarks. "Are we almost there?"

"Not too far now. About an hour," she said, blowing her nose.

"Are you all right?" I asked.

"Oh, just a little sad, I guess."

"Are you sad because of great-grandmother Ola?"

"That, too," she answered.

I wondered if she was thinking of my dad. About his leaving us. Ginny never talked about him, except to say he didn't want to fight in Vietnam. I didn't hold that against him, but as far as we were concerned, he abandoned us and he might as well be dead, too.

I didn't want to think of my great-grandmother Ola's funeral, either. Watching the road as Ginny raced through the night had scared me enough. Seems like now that we were getting closer, she was in more of a hurry. The way she swerved around a sharp turn in the road and zoomed up and down hills made me feel funny, like riding a roller coaster and leaving my stomach behind.

In a while Ginny started humming along with the music on the radio again. The Grass Roots were singing "Let's Live," and I wanted to live, that's for sure. I kind of got the feeling we might be racing to our own funeral, if she didn't slow down. "Ginny, how come you're driving so fast?"

She blinked her eyes and shook her head awake. "Josie, honey, these hills are my old stomping grounds. I'd know my way around them blindfolded. When I was little, your grandmother Louise and I came up to Granny Ola's every summer. Later, I moved up here to stay with her for a while." Ginny drove silent for a stretch of miles.

I asked her why she moved in with great-grandmother Ola, and she shrugged. "Oh, seems that I was a rebel, so mama sent me to the hills. She didn't know I could get into just as much trouble up here, but I loved roaming through the woods and riding mules with our neighbors. One time Michelle Peters hitched their mule, which was reddish brown and pretty as a horse, onto a dilapidated buckboard that Granny Ola called a Hoover cart."

"Why'd she call it that?"

"Back in Granny Ola's younger days, many people were so poor they couldn't afford to buy gasoline or the upkeep of their automobiles, so they put them on blocks to keep the tires from rotting and the metal from rusting. Then they went everywhere in a horse-drawn cart. Sometimes they removed the wheels and springs and attached their cars to a cart for better comfort. Hoover was the president of the United States then, so they named the cart after him.

"Anyway, Michelle rode over to our place, whooping and holding the reins and bouncing around that rattling cart. I jumped on and her mule trotted us down to Swan Creek. After hitching it to a tree, we shed our clothes and skinny-dipped, shivering and giggling. She was a wild thing, but we had some good times."

"Shame on you," I teased.

Ginny laughed and tickled my knee. "Nobody saw us. That was about the most fun I ever had up here. Michelle married and dropped out of high school. Never heard from her again. I did finish school, but I couldn't get out of here fast enough."

Pineridge

I didn't blame Ginny for wanting out of these hills. Every town we raced through seemed like there wasn't anything to do. No roller-skating rinks, no libraries, and just a few ice cream parlors.

As we drove up and down a hilly town named Branson, Ginny remembered that she used to bring Granny Ola here to shop for groceries and go to the washateria.

"I asked her why she wanted to drive past Forsyth to do her laundry thirty miles away, and Granny Ola sassed, 'I like driving over the mountain, that's why.'"

"Are we going to stop and eat?" I asked. We'd driven all night just snacking on chips and dry cereal.

"Hold on, sweetie, we're almost to Forsyth." When we pulled into town, Ginny stopped and bought some milk and eggs. "This town is what I remember liking best," she said.

We walked across the street and stood on a hill. A wooden sign said we were overlooking Lake Taney-como fed by the White River. "Where did they get the name for White River?"

Ginny got in her school-teacher act. "It's called White River because there's all these cold springs that feed into it. When the cold streams hit the warm river water, it makes steam. We used to camp by the river, and every morning it had a ghostly look with the foggy steam rising. All our gear would be wet. I mean dripping wet."

"Brrrr." I stared down the hill. Here it was 1967 and the old white houses still had a horse-and-buggy look, and water marks up to the windows that showed what a river can do.

We got back in the car and turned onto Pineridge scenic route. Ginny piped, "Just eight more miles, Josie, and we're there. Look for Granny Ola's mailbox with zinnias growing around it." We drove down a steep hill, and I wondered how anyone could get back up if it snowed.

At the bottom of the hill, we rushed over a creek. Ginny pointed to a rusty pipe strung down the side of the hill with water gushing out of it. "That's where Granny Ola used to get her water. We'd haul a big old barrel down here and fill it up. Took two men to help us lift it back on her pickup truck. Then she'd turn that truck around and off we'd go, winding up the hill and home. She drove in little jerky movements, always had her hands on the steering wheel, twisting it left and right. I was a nervous wreck."

"I know how she feels," I mumbled, staring out the window at a farmer already up and plowing with an old plow pulled by one of those pretty mules Ginny was talking about.

"Look, there's a mailbox with flowers around it," I yelled. "Is that it?"

"Not yet. It's a mile or two more around this curve. I guess others dressed up their boxes like Granny Ola's. Her box will be stuck down in an old milk can with handles."

We drove a few more miles, then Ginny hollered, "There it is, Josie! Granny Ola's place."

I saw the mailbox with red and yellow zinnias growing down in the ditch like wildflowers. We turned into a rutted one-lane drive through a forest of pines and redbud trees, only it was too late in the summer for redbuds, just green leaves. I recognized them because trees like that grow in our trailer park.

We stopped at a clearing in front of a shed that Ginny said covered the well. Just beyond that was a vegetable and flower garden next to an old house. The rocking chair on the stoop rocked just a little as a woman ran from the house toward Ginny.

"You've got to be Ginny. My lands, you must be tired."

"Well, yes, we are," Ginny said. "Alma, it's good to finally meet you." They stood around hugging. Ginny turned to me and said, "Josie, I want you to meet Alma, and I suppose this is your little girl, Sara. Granny Ola wrote me about her."

Alma hugged me, too, almost smothering me in her big bosom. "This is my young'un, Sara. She's ten, about your age, darling. Come on in. I know you're beat."

Ginny told her we'd get our things and follow them right in. "They live across the ridge from here," Ginny whispered. "They moved up from Mississippi a few years ago, and Granny Ola made friends with them right away."

We went inside the house, and Alma bent down and locked her large brown eyes onto mine. "Josie, baby, are you hungry, child? I cooked up some cornbread and a mess of black-eyed peas Ola and me canned."

"No, thank you," I said, making a face. Ginny used to cook a pot of peas and try to make cornbread like her Granny Ola, but I never did like either one.

Ginny cleared her throat and glared at me. She knew what I was thinking, I guess. "We'd love some peas and cornbread, Alma."

Sara sniffed her nose up at me. "They's good, even if you city folks don't think so."

I stared at her and wondered if her shiny face meant she'd been crying. I kept looking at her hair, what I could see of it. She had a zillion rags poking out of her head, each of them a different color.

"What've you got all those rags in your hair for?" I asked.

"I'm curling my hair for the funeral," she said. Then she got the plates out just like she lived there.

Alma flicked a tear from her cheek. "We're goin' to miss Ola. Ever since we moved up here and bought that place back in the woods, Ola was always our friend. She brought us fresh vegetables from her garden and canned goods every time she came calling. Seemed like she couldn't see us often enough." Ginny smiled at Alma and grabbed her hand.

I sat down at the table. A cloth covered peanut butter and jellies and hot sauce. I looked around to see if great-grandmother Ola didn't have a refrigerator. She did, but I guess she forgot to put everything in it.

"We called the coroner," Alma said. "Ola, she lay resting at the funeral parlor."

Ginny patted her on the shoulder and put a pot of coffee on. She asked Alma how they happened to find Ola.

"I come over here like me and Sara always do every morning. Sometimes we pick peas in Ola's garden, and I help her snap them. She always gave us jellies and jams. That woman was a generous soul."

Sara nodded her head, and her stiff rag tails didn't budge a hair.

"Anyway," Alma continued, "yesterday morning when we came, we found her sitting in that old overstuffed chair with her hairbrush in her lap and all the pins out. The TV blared away, and Ola sat there like she done every morning, watching her soaps and brushing that long hair of hers. But this time she was cold as old Spring Creek."

Sara whispered in a low voice, "Rocky was sittin' 'n starin' through that old raggy screen door when we came."

"Rocky?" I asked.

Sara lowered her eyes. "Old Rocky is her hound dog. He's all the time right there against the door. We never get in 'less he want us to."

Ginny laughed. "That Rocky, he was always scratching and sitting by the door. He's still here, I guess. Fleas and all."

Sara nodded. "Out chasing a squirrel, I suppose. He sort of protected Ola. She would yell, 'Git up, you lazy hound. Git away from my front door so's I can open it.' And he'd just thump his tail on the stoop, while she kept a'fussin'. 'How'm I gonna feed you if you lay around all day?' she'd say."

Alma and Ginny laughed, so Sara kept talking. "He

always was a'scratchin' at his fleas, just like her hens scratch in the garden. Scratch. Scratch. Scratching all day."

I looked at Sara. At first I thought maybe I could learn to like her. She was cute and said funny things. But then she said something that made me feel strange.

"Miss Ola was my best friend."

All at once she started crying over my great-grandmother Ola. How could she cry when I didn't feel like crying at all?

And who did she think she was, acting like it was *her* great-grandmother who died?

The Cabin

After Alma and Sara left, I plopped into Ola's old overstuffed chair, where she was sitting when Alma and Sara found her. Dust swooshed up and danced in streaks of afternoon sunlight shining through the cracked windowpane.

I could feel the chair's warm arms circle around me. No wonder Ola had liked it. I picked up a mint out of a dusty pink glass bowl off the coffee table, but it stuck to all the other mints. I pried one off with my teeth, getting my fingers sticky. "Everything sure is hot," I murmured. "Aren't there any fans around here?"

"We'll cool off. Just be calm," Ginny said.

She pulled her wavy red hair up off her neck. Hair so bright it looked like it was on fire. Why'd I have to have mousy blond hair?

We wandered into Ola's sitting room with the fireplace. There was enough junk on the mantel to start a flea market. Thimbles, crochet needles, and dirty white thread. Two old lamps made of oiled paper had a round, pink rose painted on each side of the shades. The kind that might have been in the Romeo and Juliet movie I saw on Mrs. Reynolds' TV. And rocks! "Ginny, look. Great-grandmother Ola collected rocks just like me."

I gazed around the room, full of faded pictures and dried flower arrangements. Magazines and letters announcing big prize contests cluttered everything. There wasn't even a place to sit on the couch. "Why did she keep all this stuff?"

"I guess Granny Ola figured on winning the jackpot one day," Ginny answered, sifting through the junk mail. "All these promises to win big money. I don't think she ever threw any of them away." Ginny shook her head. "Granny Ola sure wasn't much of a housekeeper." She handed a duster to me and walked into the next room.

"Is this a hint?" I asked, knowing the answer all the same.

I was flicking off dust around the room when I found a little harp-shaped piece of metal. "What's this?"

Ginny popped her head around the door. "Look at that! It's Granny Ola's juice harp. She always carried it with her."

"What'd she do with it?"

"She played it," Ginny said, as she took it from me. "Like this." She held it in her left hand, parted her lips, and put the harp next to her teeth. Then she strummed on it with her fingers. It made a twanging sound.

"Let me try." I did what she did, and when I thumped my finger on the harp, it bit my lip. Sent sharp pains through my teeth, too. "Ouch! That hurts. Why would she always have it with her?" I held my mouth and handed it back to Ginny.

"It pleased her. I remember one time I went with Granny Ola to the county fair. She had fried some apple pies and put me in charge of selling them. When I next found her, she was sitting on top of the picnic table playing that little harp in time to the western band music on the stage. She was so cute with her bonnet and her hose rolled down to her ankles, tapping her foot and thumping away. She even went up on the stage and played with the band for a number or two."

Ginny dropped the harp in her pocket and smiled. "Come on, Josie, let's get ready. It's time to go to Granny Ola's wake." She straightened her hair and smeared on some lipstick.

I brushed off my jeans and washed my hands in the kitchen sink. Then I dashed the cold water on my neck, trying to cool down. At least this house has running water.

After I tidied up, we headed for our car. "Take care of Granny Ola's place, Rocky," Ginny yelled.

He growled and muttered a woof. Mangy old dog, I thought.

⌒⁀⌒

On the way to the funeral home, Ginny explained what a wake was. "It's where people gather before a funeral and console one another and view the loved one. A long time ago, people didn't have funeral homes, so neighbors and family members would sit up with the body at night, keeping watch over it."

"Were they afraid it would be stolen?" I asked.

"No," Ginny said with a laugh, "but it was something friends could do for the bereaved family. Show respect and all."

This got me thinking about our family. Great-grandmother Ola was my grandma Louise's mama, and Louise was Ginny's mama, and Ginny was my mama. "We go on and on, I guess," I said quietly.

Ginny nodded. "That's right."

There wasn't much traffic on the road, but we could see pickups and cars with flat tires set back in the trees. Most of the houses were wood-framed like Ola's. But occasionally we'd pass a log cabin. "Look, Ginny. Look at that house."

"That's Ted Gilmer's. Built it himself. He cut those pine logs down in the holler and got his mules to drag them up the hill. Remember what a hexagon is?"

"Yeah, a six-sided something or other."

"Well, he cut those logs into hexagons and laid them on top of each other with those thin white strips of wood in between. I used to watch him building it when I was in high school. Built his wife that pretty house, but didn't pipe in water. She still had to catch rain in a cistern and buy water off a truck."

"How did great-grandmother Ola finally get her running water?" I asked.

Ginny studied a minute. "I know it was when

grandpa was alive. He had a deep well dug, then piped pure cold water inside the house."

"Why do you call that little cabin a house?"

"Josie, if Granny Ola ever heard you call her home a cabin, she'd just about wallop you."

"Wallop me?"

"Yeah, I guess I get to using my old-timey sayings up here."

"Just something about this place."

We passed a picnic park with a bunch of motor-cyclists having a party. I thought how much fun it would be to ride a bike around the smooth curves in the road and up and down the hills. Tall pine trees shaded us from the sunlight. Ginny pointed to her high school as we went through a tiny town named Chadwick. "Grades one through twelve all bunched together."

Ola's Wake

We rolled into a little town called Ozark. The funeral home was halfway down the hill, and Ginny had to swerve real quick to the left. She steered our old car in for a landing, right next to the entrance. My hands felt cold and sweaty as we walked inside. I wasn't sure I could look at a dead person.

The sweet smell of flowers filled the air as we walked through the parlor. A nice woman asked if she could help. Ginny told her that we were there to see Mrs. Ola Jones.

We followed her to the room where Ola lay resting

inside a silver and brass casket, lined with pink satin. I could see part of Ola's face from the door, but since I had never seen a person all laid out like that, I couldn't move closer.

Everything was quiet except for the organ music. Ginny walked over and peered down inside at her Granny Ola. I looked at all the flowers in baskets and plastic cans covered with pink foil.

Finally, I moved toward Ginny and put my hands on the edge of the casket. I saw an old woman with deep lines around her eyes and mouth. She had kind of a satisfied look on her face, or was that a grin? I couldn't tell, not ever knowing her. I shivered even though I wasn't cold. "She looks older than her pictures."

Ginny put her arm around me. "She does look older than the last time I saw her. Her red and silver hair shines like a halo. She always pushed that wave in at her forehead with two fingers," Ginny said.

I pictured her combing her long hair and pushing

a big wave in. I guess she was particular about how she looked. I wished I could have known her when she was alive. I bet I would have loved her more than Sara does.

"I brought you by once when you were just a little baby, Josie. We drove all the way down that old winding mountain to see her. Twisting roads, banked high with snow. Tree branches bent down heavy with ice. It was a frozen tunnel."

"I don't remember it," I said, moving away from Ginny and the casket. Ginny followed after me.

"Every time I spoke to her over the phone or got a letter from her, she talked about how her sweet baby came to see her. Granny Ola only saw you that one time, but she always remembered you. She liked that big dimple on your cheek, and she loved making you giggle. She would get on the floor and bray a big mule *hee-haw*. You would cackle out loud, like your tickle box was turned over."

Ginny's voice got quieter. "All her friends say she

was more fun than riding sidesaddle on a donkey." Tears brimmed in her eyes, but when some of Ola's neighbors came in, Ginny brushed the tears away. Everybody shook hands and hugged and patted each other.

Sara stood in the doorway, clutching an old doll in her arms. I stared at her and she stared back with those brown eyes big as dinner plates. Finally, I said, "Well, come on in."

At first she kept staring at me, sulky-like. Then she ambled inside the room.

"Can I hold your doll?" I asked. When she jerked her hand toward me, I took the doll and looked at it real close. It was so old and ugly, I almost dropped it.

"What's this?"

"A doll. Miss Ola gave it to me," Sara said. "She made it out of a dried-up apple."

I peered down into that apple head face. "It looks dead."

"Give it here!" Sara demanded, trying to take it back.

I kept staring at it. All I could think of was that I never got a doll from my great-grandmother, ugly or not. I gave the doll back to Sara. She ran over to her mama.

Not knowing anybody except Alma and Sara, I stood alone next to some palms by the casket. Ginny kept busy talking to everyone, saying, "How've you been?" and "It's so good to see you." It was odd seeing all these people in the same room with a dead person, and them just visiting away.

I wished I could talk to Ola and get to know her. There she was all laid out in her pretty pink bed, looking like she was asleep in her best clothes and with lipstick on. She wore a blue silk suit. I could tell it wasn't new, but it looked nice. I sniffed at one of the red roses spilling from the top of the casket.

Alma peeked over my shoulder. "Your mama bought that suit for her Granny Ola last year at a used clothing store, and sent it to her. Ola never liked anything brand-new. She always told Ginny to wear the new off before she sent her anything." While everyone visited with each other, I kept staring at Ola's little thin lips and straight nose. Just like Ginny's. I wished my nose was shaped like theirs.

More people came down the hall looking for us. Ginny spoke to a man named Harvey, steering him toward the casket. He leaned on a cane and held Sara's hand, so I figured he was her daddy. I pushed the palms aside and hid behind them.

Sara let go of his hand and stood right in front of me. She hugged her dried-up crinkled doll just to make me jealous, I bet.

Alma held on to Ginny's arm. I thought she was going to cry, but instead she laughed right out loud.

Sara and I both jumped.

"Oh, that Ola," Alma said, wiping her eyes. "I had adventuresome times with that woman. And I'll never forget when we went berry picking."

For a second I thought I saw a corner of Ola's lips curl in a stiff little smirk. I thought it would be funny if she could hear us.

More friends of Ola's gathered around the casket. Some cried. Others listened to Alma tell her story.

Berries and a Bear

"Well sir'ee," Alma began, "one time me and Ola rode over to Gravoity Mills where you know the wild raspberries bloom early in June." Friends standing around listening to Alma nodded.

I moved a palm leaf over just a bit so I could see better. Seemed as though I could hear better if I could see, but that Sara just moved right in front of me again.

"Pssst!" I said. But she clutched that old doll and listened to her mama.

"Ola knew a place no one ever went, so there

oughta be plenty of berries to pick. That morning I took Harvey's old pickup truck and ran by Ola's place. I had a thermos of coffee and she jumped in with a sack lunch. The truck rattled down a wagon road used by them foresters. Later, we parked in a clearing where the trees had been cut down.

"We were hurrying along and then Ola stopped for a bit. She'd found a young willow tree with strong branches, and just like a kid she climbed on that little tree branch, and jumped up and down, like it were a willow seesaw. Then we walked over the hill till we found that berry patch.

"After we'd picked several quarts of juicy raspberries, I sat on a tree stump and rested my bones. Ola perched herself on a rock and took her juice harp out and started thumping away.

"I told Ola I was getting hungry, but right then she spied more ripe berries just a ways down the hill. I watched Ola push the bushes back with her crooked cane and creep up on that new berry patch. She started singing, 'Shall we gather at the river.' Singing and picking berries."

Sara still kept herself right in front of me. Standing on one foot, then the other, never leaving the spot.

Alma continued, "Then I smelt something real strong. Well, I've been in these woods long enough to know what I smelt was a bear!"

"A bear?" I cried out. Everyone turned around and stared at me.

"That's right, child. A bear. Sometimes they wander down through our woods. I knew Ola would throw a hissy fit if I told her I smelled a bear, so I whispered real gentle-like, 'Ola, we got enough berries now. Come on, let's git.'

"She sassed me, snippety as a puppy pulling on a shoestring: 'Hold your horses, Alma. I want some of these plump berries over here.'

" 'Hurry up,' I told her. Why, I could hear the bear's footsteps in the leaves.

"I finally grabbed Ola by the elbow and pulled her back up the hill. I had three full buckets, and I thought they'd be the last berries I'd ever see, if that bear got us.

"Ola got angry with me, complaining and chewing me out, but I finally coached her back to the truck, and she propped her buckets on the hood. I'll be bamboozled if she didn't take time to pull out a tissue and blow her nose. She truly was the most exasperating woman I ever knew!"

"She was always nice to me," Sara said, pulling on one of her zillion rag tails.

Just then I felt like snarling at Sara, but Alma kept talking.

"Stubborn don't describe Ola none at all," Alma said. "I jumped into the cab and slammed the door just in time to see that brown bear coming up the path. 'Ola!' I yelled. 'Get in the truck.' But always slow and obstinate as a mule, she dawdled.

"Finally, she hefted herself into the truck, and

when that stinking bear growled, Ola looked up in surprise. Well, like I figured, she threw those berries all over the seats and screamed and stomped her feet on the floorboard.

" 'Alma!' she cried. 'A bear!'

"All that time I kept trying to get the keys into the ignition. I could see that bear tromping right on, with us sitting there in that old truck, the windows stuck halfway down.

" 'What're we gonna do?' Ola fretted.

" 'Throw out our sandwiches,' I yelled.

" 'Our sandwiches?'

" '*Now!*' I said. Well, she did finally. And I turned Harvey's truck around and spun those wheels so hard we dug ruts deep as the Grand Canyon. Whew! We got out of there, but those raspberries, mixed with our sweat and fear, never did get eaten. We were so stained with red, a person might've thought we killed ourselves."

Alma sounded like she was angry, but she smiled

down at Ola lying all serene in her pink satin casket. "We never did go berry picking again after that."

"I went with her once," Sara mumbled.

Her saying that she had been berry picking with Ola made my chest hurt. I pinched her leg, and didn't even feel sorry when she squealed out.

~

Before leaving, Alma walked over to the casket and touched Ola's hand. Then she wiped her eyes, and she and Harvey hugged Ginny.

"You girls will be all right. We'll see you at the funeral tomorrow," Harvey said with a sad smile.

"Good night," Ginny said. "I appreciate your coming." Then she looked down at Sara. "You'll have to come over and play with Josie after the funeral. Will you do that?"

Sara hugged her ugly doll tight and looked at me real serious. "She probably doesn't want to, Ginny," I said.

"Why do you call your mama 'Ginny'?" Sara asked.

I looked at her straight in the eyes and tightened my lips. " 'Cause that's her name."

Ginny put her hand on my shoulder and squeezed it in the way she warns me when I've upset her.

After she told all of Ola's friends goodbye, it was just the two of us left. Ginny walked around the room, smelled the flowers and read all the cards. Then she sighed and sat down in one of the velvet-covered chairs.

I sat down beside her. "Ola was funny, wasn't she?"

"Yes, very. Independent, I guess. I don't know how you would describe her, Josie. I never figured her out myself. She was something else." She circled her arms around me. "Sometimes it's hard to know someone."

"I like her," I said. "I want to know more about her. Was she really as stubborn as Alma said? I want to know her better than Sara does."

Ginny laughed and stood up. "I noticed how you and Sara were acting. What are we going to do about you two?"

Cousin Zack

"Someone just walked in," Ginny said. "I'll go see who it is." Ginny gently touched my ear as she left the room.

For the first time, I was alone with great-grandmother Ola. It felt kind of spooky, but I wanted to get acquainted with her. I eased over to the casket and watched her for a while. I tried to picture her holding me when I was a baby. I'll bet if I had come up here more often, I would have gone berry picking with her, too. She could have shown me around the woods, and we would have found all kinds of things. Bird's nests. Rabbit holes. Rocks smooth as glass.

She looked just like she was sleeping. "Ola," I whispered, "can you hear me?

"Did you really throw your lunch to a bear? Ola, I'm your great-granddaughter, Josie. Maybe you know me as Josephine. Remember when I came to see you? I was just a baby in diapers, so I can't remember, but Ginny told me about it. She drove us up here in the ice and snow."

Ola lay there real quiet and didn't nod or open her eyes. I wanted to touch her hand, just as Alma had done. But I couldn't. When I heard someone else coming in the room, I moved back to the palms and crouched down again.

Ginny had her hand through a tall man's arm. "I'm so happy you're here, Zack. Where you living these days?"

"I've been on the road with my band. Heard about Ola over in Branson. Never figured she'd leave us.

"Heck, you look prettier than a sunset."

Ginny's face got red. "How long has it been since we've seen each other?"

"Long time. 'Bout ten years, I reckon."

"What with work and Josie's schooling, I just—"

"No need explainin', cousin. We all know how that goes. Time does have a way of passin'."

Zack called Ginny "cousin" so I guess we did have a relative after all. He wore a big white cowboy hat and a string bow tie. His boots were real shiny.

Zack looked down at Ola. "She sure was a fine lady." He rubbed his chin and laughed.

"What're you laughing at?" I asked.

"Who said that?" Zack parted the palms, and there I sat like a monkey grinning through bars. "Why, lookee here. Who's this sweet little thing, Ginny?"

"This is my daughter, Josie. Zack is a distant cousin, Josie."

"I guess you knew my great-grandmother Ola better'n me, too, didn't you?"

Zack just patted my head softly. "Josie, darling, I'm sorry you missed out on one of the most talented and beloved women up in these hills." As if hearing that made me feel any better.

Then we heard a lot of loud talking and two gangly men wearing scruffy jeans and twisting their dirty felt hats in their hands crept into the room. Neither one had any hair.

Zack put his hand out for a shake. "Why if it isn't Hank and Hooter. How you boys been?"

"Just middlin'," Hank said. "Just middlin'. Can't complain much though. We're alive, ain't we?" He laughed and Hooter snorted, just shaking his head.

"You remember Ginny, Ola's granddaughter, don't you?" Hank and Hooter smiled and said they remembered, and Ginny shook their hands. Then Zack introduced me. "This is Josie, Ginny's daughter."

They stared at me wide-eyed. Hooter said, "I declare, Hank, don't she beat all? Looks just like Ola."

"Yep, like an itty-bitty Ola," Hank said. Before the clock ticked a minute, they started telling stories, too. They talked so loud you wouldn't think we were all in a funeral parlor.

"Remember, Hooter, that time we'd been fishing and decided to come by Ola's and see if she had any fresh fried apple pies for the bake sale?"

I scooted in closer to listen. "Yeah," Hooter answered. "That Ola made the best fried pies on the ridge. She was always giving them away. People would drop in, and she'd see that they had something in their bellies before they left."

"We found her out there chasing that big hog around the garden," Hank said. "Had that crooked stick she always went exploring the place with."

He slapped Hooter on the back and continued, "Ola yelled, 'Git outta my garden!' and she chased that boar into the woods and back. She stayed right behind it, heading for the pen. She had it almost corralled when the both of them fell smack into a muddy pig waller. Ola got so mad, I thought she'd have a hog-killing right there in the summertime."

Both men doubled up laughing. "Mud dribbled down her face. In her eyes and mouth. I never heard such colorful phrasing coming from a woman," Hank said. "Before long, she was laughing at herself, though."

Ginny didn't laugh, and I didn't like hearing about Ola falling in a muddy waller.

Hooter kept talking. "Guess that was why Ola had so much fun at the fall slaughter. Gettin' even with that old boar. She invited everyone over for roast pig, and gave them what was left. That was a fine party, yes sir'ee."

"I declare, Hank," Hooter said, looking at me again, "don't she beat all? Just like Ola used to be."

"Josie looks a lot like Ola, all righty," Zack said. Then he took them by the arms. "Boys, it was great seeing you. Thanks for coming by." He walked them out the door, into the hall, and onto the road. I could hear them laughing and talking loud all the way out.

It was late in the evening, and Ginny asked Zack if he was coming to the funeral tomorrow.

"Sure am. Do you want me to pick you up?"

"Please do." Ginny looked relieved to have that settled.

Zack put his arm around Ginny and me. "Good night, pretty cousins. See you in the morning."

I couldn't keep from smiling thinking how Zack included me in being pretty. Of course, he'd say that about Ginny 'cause she's beautiful. But I decided I liked meeting a cousin and hearing compliments.

"Hank and Hooter talk funny. Why do folks talk different up here?" I asked.

Ginny smiled and hugged me. "I went to a lot of trouble to quit that kind of talk, Josie. It doesn't set well when you're trying to find a job and you sound like a hillbilly." Then she took Ola's little harp out of her pocket and wiped it with her skirt. She walked over to the casket and smiled down at Ola, and then put the harp on the pink satin coverlet next to her hands.

"Was Ola a hillbilly?"

Ginny thought for a minute. "Over the years she molded herself to whatever she felt like. I remember when she joined a service club, she wore a beautiful white taffeta evening dress to some sort of doings. She sure didn't look like a hillbilly then. But living by herself so long and up in these hills, a person sinks into the country way of life, I reckon."

Ginny was beginning to sink a little, I thought. "I want to tell Ola goodbye before we go."

"Okay," she said. "See you in a bit."

I eased back over to the casket. Before I knew it, I was talking away. "Ola, I didn't care for those two guys laughing at you and that pig. But I really did like that story Ginny told me today about you playing your juice harp with the band. I wish I could have been there to see you on that stage. I always wanted to perform at school, but we moved around so much I never got to try out. I play a harmonica pretty good. I tried to play your juice harp today, but it stung my lips and zinged my teeth. It almost gave me a blister."

I reached down and touched her hand, then drew it back real quick. I thought it would be soft, but it wasn't. It felt kind of like petrified wood.

The Shower Bath

Ginny drove us home from the funeral parlor. She put her arm around me as I snuggled up to her, and I thought of all the funny things I had heard about Ola today.

I stared out at the rutted road. Bugs and all sorts of fluttery things lit up in the Cadillac headlights. My eyelids drooped, and my chin bobbed up and down on my chest. I dozed until Ginny woke me up giggling over something.

"What's so funny?" I asked.

That made Ginny laugh again. She snickered and

got her laugh caught in her nose, and it came out sounding like a goose honking. "Oh," she said, pushing me up, "I was laughing about the time I was a teenager visiting up here, and Zack took Granny Ola and me into Forsyth for groceries.

"Well, Granny Ola didn't get into town often, so she had to check every nook and cranny on the square to buy some trinket for me."

"I know she likes trinkets," I piped up. "I saw lots of them in her bedroom."

Ginny continued, "Lord knows, I didn't need any little junky souvenir, but it made her happy to buy something for me. One time she bought a rose rock. It was rusty red and rough, like lava rock. Had a rose fragrance for a while. I put it in that little curio box inside the trailer."

"I've seen it," I said. "All wrinkled like a dried prune."

"Yes. Anyway, she bought one for Zack, too. I remember he dropped his into his pocket and said he'd always keep it to remind him of Ola."

"Aren't you going to tell me what was so funny?"

"Well, one day we drove over to the lookout off the highway. We stood there peering down at Lake Taneycomo, and Granny Ola said she'd like to buy a house down by that river. 'But you know,' she'd argue with herself, 'it floods just about every time it rains. Like to build me a two-story brick home right on the bank. Then it could flood all it wanted to. I'd hang out the upstairs windows fishing with a long line.' "

"Did she like to fish?" I asked.

"I think Granny Ola liked to do anything that was outdoors," Ginny said. "By the time we could drag her home, the ice cream was melted and her cold drinks were 'just right for drinking,' as she would say. Then she asked Zack and me to bring in the rest of the groceries while she got into something cooler. But hot as it was and our clothes plastered to us, I turned on the water at the well and sprayed Zack till his soaked shirt and pants clung like wilted grape leaves. Then he grabbed the hose and really soaked me."

Ginny laughed just telling the story until she started hiccuping. She turned into Ola's lane and rumbled through the pine trees and came to a stop in front of the cabin. "I bet that was funny, you two taking a shower bath," I said.

"Well, that was a sight seeing Zack dripping wet, but your granny . . . We were having a good time running around soaking wet, squealing and whooping as we splashed each other. We forgot she had asked us to bring in the groceries.

"All of a sudden, here comes Granny Ola. She burst through the screen door as if she were a hen chasing a cricket. She headed for the car, grabbed those two heavy sacks of groceries, and took them in herself."

I frowned. "What's so funny about that?"

"Well," Ginny said, "she had taken off her clothes and run outside in her underwear."

"Her underwear?"

"Yeah, in her underwear. She had her hose

rolled down to her ankles, just as she always wore them. And her little flat breasts flopping in an old bra."

"I wish I could've been there to see Ola in her underwear."

Ginny quit laughing. "We told her she should come and take a shower bath with us, but she said she'd catch a cold. Kinda like how you catch colds easily, too, Josie."

Ginny had tears in her eyes. I thought she might start crying, but she just slumped down in the seat and stayed in the car. "I'd like to sit here a bit, Josie, and cool off." She stared out into the night, the lights from over the well shed beaming down on her face. "It must be fixing to storm."

I got out of the car and played with Rocky. All at once, thunder rolled through the hills and lightning split the sky in half. Before we could get inside, rain poured down and soaked us.

"Whew! That came fast," Ginny said. "Let's get

out of our wet clothes and clear this junk off the couch, so you can have a place to sleep."

"Feels good," I said, loving the chill. I changed T-shirts and put on dry underwear.

Ginny unfolded the couch and spread some old musty quilts to pad the worn mattress and soften the springs poking through. She found some sheets still in the package marked $2.98. "Look at this, Josie. Can't get good sheets for this price anymore. Granny Ola liked pretty things, but she saved them for something special. I guess we're special enough."

She tucked me in, and I felt cozy lying close to Ola's chair. The place where she spent so much time watching her soaps and reading her mail. I wondered what Ola was like when she was my age. "Ginny, when you were a little girl, what did you and Ola do?"

"Oh, we walked in the woods and gathered mushrooms. All kinds, Josie. Granny Ola recognized real delicacies, like Poor Man's Beef Steak. It looks a little like a piece of liver."

"I hate liver," I said.

"Well, I don't much like it, either, but I'm not talking about liver, just a mushroom that looks like it. Anyway, I went with her one time into town where she sold them at a grocery store. The grocer man said that he'd buy all she could find. She really was resourceful. Selling to the grocer, frying delicious pies, crocheting doilies and coverlets. She scratched out a living just fine."

"Like her hens?" I asked, thinking how Sara had described them. "Always a'scratching in her garden?"

Ginny laughed. "Something like that." She turned out the light and whispered, "Sleep tight."

Digging for Potatoes

I wished I could have hunted wild plants with Ola like Ginny did. Then that little Sara popped into my mind. She more than likely gathered mushrooms with Ola, too.

I tried to go to sleep, but it rained hard and kept me awake. Lightning lit up the room and all the old pictures on the wall seemed to grin and laugh. I hid my face under the covers, but I couldn't breathe, it was so musty and warm. I peeked out from the quilt and the room zoomed up and down like an elevator. The faded wallpaper came alive with figures of little old ladies dressed in bakers' uniforms and old-fashioned bonnets. They were jumping out of a biscuit can and rolling in their own dough. When I closed my eyes, they went away.

Later the rain poured through the roof onto my face. Every so often a big drip . . . drip . . . splattered my eyelids. I turned my pillow to the other end of the couch so I couldn't see the pictures. Then only my feet got wet.

I must have finally fallen asleep, because the next morning sticky matter sealed my eyes shut. I could hardly swallow, and every time I coughed, my head ached. Even my eyeballs were sore. I wanted to get up, but I didn't feel like crawling off the couch.

Ginny came in with a washcloth and a pitcher of warm water. "Here, sweets, wash your face, and you'll feel better."

I washed my face and unstuck my eyes. When I stood up, the room spun around like a whirlpool. I needed to go to the bathroom, so I grabbed hold of the wall and furniture, until I made it in there. It was a little closet tacked onto the house, but at least it was inside and had running water.

The rain had cooled the heat, but the sun sparkling through the pine trees hurt my eyes. I shivered through breakfast and couldn't eat a thing. The strawberries Ginny found in Ola's freezer looked like they had black ants on them.

"You love strawberries, Josie. Won't you try some?" When I shook my head, she said that maybe I oughtn't go to the funeral.

"I have to go," I cried. "I won't ever see Ola again if I don't."

Ginny looked at me funny. "I didn't think you wanted to go." She put her cool hand on my forehead. "I'm worried about you," she said.

"I'll be all right."

"We'll see how you feel in an hour."

Later, I pulled on my jeans, combed my matted hair, and cleared the breakfast table. My eyeballs still felt sore, but I didn't let on. I kept quiet, too, so I wouldn't cough. I even dug my cards out of my suit-case and tried to play a game of solitaire.

Ginny went outside and asked me to bring her a pan and an old fork. She said the fresh air would do me good.

I found a bent-up fork and an old pan under the kitchen sink. It seemed like most of Ola's pots were old and bent, just like her, I guess. I took them out to Ginny.

"I want you to see how Granny Ola took a fork and, just like magic, dug up a potato!"

Ginny scratched around in the dirt, and all I could see was some rocks and sand. "I don't know how you're gonna find a potato down in that dirt." But she did. She poked the fork right into a little red potato and handed it to me. I put it in the pan and waited for her to find another one. She found a few more.

"Let me dig some." For a moment I forgot how bad I felt and I scratched around like Ginny did with the fork.

"When I was your age," Ginny said, "I thought it was a miracle how my Granny Ola could dig here and there and come up with a potato. Of course, now I know that these old green plants have potatoes on their roots."

I found a potato about the size of a radish, but when I tried to get up and show Ginny, my knees wobbled. I felt dizzy as the garden spun around in my head.

Ginny pulled me up and put her hands on my forehead. "My Lord, Josie, you're burning up." I dropped the potatoes, and we stumbled toward the screen door.

When we got to Ola's bed, I fell facedown on it. I imagined I could smell her. Since I hadn't ever been around Ola, I really didn't know what she smelled like. But as I lay there in that cocoon of quilts and her nightgown that I found under her pillow, I really could smell her.

Ginny tucked the covers around me and went to the kitchen. I kicked the quilts off, but when I heard the faucet running the well water, I shivered. When she placed the cool rag on my forehead, I felt a chill throughout my body. My teeth started to chatter, and I shook so hard my bones seemed to dance. I pulled the quilts up over my head.

✺

Ginny went to Ola's funeral without me. When Alma and Harvey and Sara came by, I heard Ginny ask if Sara could stay behind.

"Why sure she can," Alma said. "You don't mind, do you, baby?"

Sara took one look at me and squeezed her doll. I could tell without her saying so that she didn't want to stay. She went into the other room and sat down in Ola's dusty chair to sulk.

"I really appreciate this," Ginny said. "Harvey, you and Alma can ride with Zack and me." Ginny bent down and touched my cheek. "We'll be back soon, Josie."

They drove off, and I lay flat on Ola's bed, unable

to lift my head. I guess I was just as angry about missing Ola's funeral as Sara. But I ignored her and stared at the pictures hanging on the faded wallpaper. One of Ola when she was real young looked down at me and smiled. I smiled back, then Sara wet the washrag again and put it over my face. I couldn't see the picture anymore, except in my mind. My eyes were heavy, and the cold rag felt good. I quit shivering and dozed off.

Shaking the Rafters

I must have slept on and off. I know I kicked at the covers, but Sara kept pulling them up. My throat burned and my body ached something fierce. Then a comfort feeling settled over me.

❧

I could see Ola coming out of the picture. She was surrounded by a bright light. Then she kind of drifted toward me. At first, I was scared. You're dead, aren't you? I thought.

Then Ola held out her hand and smiled at me like

she did in the picture. I took her hand and suddenly felt myself rising up, almost floating, over the end of the bed. I took slow-motion strides beside her, as she drifted to the kitchen. Ola picked up the lid on the pot of green beans and tasted them. She smacked her lips and snipped, "That Ginny! Never used enough salt. She has too many newfangled ideas about what's good for you."

I remembered Ginny saying that Ola never thought other people's cooking was salty enough. So there she was, doctoring up the beans to suit herself at her own funeral dinner. And I was with her. I was with Ola!

Then we moved through the screen door, and I saw Ginny spreading a long, red-checked tablecloth over Ola's battered picnic table. "The day smiled down on us and made it perfect for a picnic. I like picnics," Ola said.

"Me, too," I added. Then as we rushed past, Ola pulled me toward the tall pine trees and scrubby oaks.

Now and then, she would jump over a culvert, holding me like a kite fluttering in the breeze.

We slowed down and walked through the forest. Every once in a while Ola lifted a rock or turned up a leaf. "What're you looking for, Ola?"

She put her hands on her hips and stared at me. "Ola! You are a mite sassy to be calling me by my first name, young'un. I'll thank you if you show some respect. You ask what I was looking for? Berries, what else?"

I'd never thought I was being disrespectful to her by calling her by her first name, but I guess she thought so. She kept pushing away leaves and looking under them where bugs and spiders clustered. Then she kicked at another drift of plants. "What about mushrooms?" I asked.

"Nope," Ola said in a spitfire kind of way. "Usually find them north side of a tree."

We ran on like we were in a hurry, and once in a while we stopped so Ola could check out a rock or look under a berry bush. The next thing I knew, we were at a little church on the side of a hill with trees all around. I noticed two outhouses sitting on the edge of the sloping yard.

Singing floated out through the windows. We swooped up the steps and into the church full of people. Ola and me sat down on a hard bench in the back row. Up front sat Ginny, Zack, Harvey, and Alma, and a bunch of strangers. I guess they weren't strangers to Ola, though. Then I spotted the pink-lined casket with velvet red roses standing in the middle of the aisle down front. Wildflowers decorated the top of the piano and the windowsills. It seemed funny for Ola to be sitting with me and be up there in her casket, too.

The preacher talked about what a good person Ola had been and how much he enjoyed her singing. "Why," he said, "when she sang, you could hear her clear 'cross the county line. That country alto of hers added to our worship services every Sunday." Someone in the church said, "Amen." Someone else giggled, then snorted and blew her nose. Ola nodded her head and applauded, but nobody turned around to see who it was.

Then the preacher said for all of us to turn to number forty-six in the hymnbook. "We should all be thankful for the many blessings that Ola has given us over the years. She surely was a generous woman. Now let's sing!"

The pianist played with her eyes closed. "She's blind as a bat," Ola whispered. "Can't see a thing, but she can play that piano." I couldn't see how she could play, being blind, but her hands flew up and down that keyboard making music.

We all sang "Count Your Blessings," and Ola, just like the preacher said, lifted her voice up to the rafters of that church. It made the windows rattle. Seemed my ears did, too. But I joined in with her. She looked down at me and shook her head. "Shh, you're off-key and too loud."

She thought I was singing too loud, but I thought she was louder. I half expected everyone to turn around to see where all the voices were coming from, but they didn't. They nodded their heads and stomped time to the music and sang joyfully. It was a mighty fine funeral.

Outside the church, people crowded around Ginny, and hugged her and patted her on the back, saying how much she looked like her Granny Ola, and how they would miss her. I thought they ought to say how much I favored her, too, but they didn't.

Ginny thanked them. "You all come by her place for dinner after the burial, you hear?"

I stood close to Ginny and tried to tell her I was there, but she never did turn around. She must not have noticed me, because she got in a car with the preacher and Zack, and they drove off. It seemed like no one at the funeral noticed me or Ola.

Ola smiled and took my hand. We turned onto a

path through the woods. "Come on, Josephine, I've got something to show you."

Farther down the path, she pointed toward a tree trunk. She pushed some moldy leaves away. "See what you can find," she said.

I bent down and saw something that looked like a bloody piece of liver.

"It's a mushroom. Some people call it Poor Man's Beef Steak," Ola said.

"Yuck!" I snapped. Ginny told me about this, but it still startled me.

Ola looked at me like I didn't have any sense, then she grinned and said, "It's a delicacy."

This is what I've been wanting to do, I thought. Find mushrooms with my great-grandmother Ola. I couldn't believe I was tromping through the forest with her doing exactly what I had hoped to do.

The way Ola flounced ahead reminded me of how Alma had said she was snippety as a puppy. I kept bouncing up and down in a moon boot stomp, wondering where we were going. Then I saw her pick up a crooked limb and use it as a walking stick to push back rocks and weeds. It looked like the one in her cabin. She must've kept that same stick all these years.

Ola didn't look back at me anymore until she came to a big patch of huckleberries. "My favorite berry, Josephine. Makes the best muffins, but I like raspberries for jelly. You should taste my prize-winning jelly."

I picked handfuls of berries and stuffed them in my pockets. Ola smiled and beckoned me to follow, so I flopped along behind her. Then she took me to the most amazing tree, and pulled away some brambles. She grabbed hold of one of its limbs that bent down when she pulled on it. "This is a willow tree, Josephine." She lifted her skirt and put her leg over it and motioned for me to climb on behind her. Just like straddling a horse, one in front and one in back, I wrapped my arms around her waist. She was warm and so skinny, I could feel her bones. She kicked the ground real gentle-like, and we went up, then came down. Up, then down. She had made a one-man see-saw, only there were two of us on one end.

Ola got off and held me on while I kicked the ground. "Whoa, this is fun," but then I kicked the ground too hard and flew up in the air. "Help!" I cried. "Help. It's too high!"

Tea Time

I felt the cool washrag on my face again. Someone kept smoothing back my hair. When I opened my eyes, I saw Sara all dressed in white staring down at me with her eyebrows scrunched together. Then a smile crinkled up her face. "Ginny!" Sara yelled. "Come look at Josie."

Ginny rushed up to me in Ola's bed and bent down and kissed my wet face. Alma peeked into the room. "What's the matter, Sara?"

"Josie's better, Alma," Ginny cried. "Just feel. She's cooled off."

They stared down at me with tears in their eyes. Ginny hugged me and covered me up some more, but I wanted to get up. "Oh, Josie, we've been so worried. The doctor came out here and left some medicine. He said to let you rest. I was ready to take you to the hospital."

Sara crawled up on the foot of the bed. "You've been asleep all yesterday and all last night," she said.

"You mean the funeral's over?"

"Yes," Sara answered. "And what were you doing, 'up and down' and 'too high'?"

"The willow tree. Ola and me went up and down on the willow tree."

Sara looked at me wild-eyed.

I sat up and looked out the window. "Ginny, did you see Ola?"

"Oh, Josie. It was a special funeral. I'm sorry you weren't there. So many people brought flowers from their yards and set them around the church."

"I saw the flowers and heard the singing. But I

meant did you see her outside in the yard, talking to those people?"

Ginny and Alma looked puzzled. "You've been sick, Josie," Ginny said.

Alma patted my forehead. "I think you'd better rest more, baby. I'm gonna make you some tea outta Ola's herb collection. She has some of that hyssop that'll cure a horse with a bad case of the hiccups."

I threw the covers back and tried to get up. The room swirled around me, and I almost fell off the bed. I struggled to put my feet on the floor. "I've been with Ola," I said. "We were at the funeral. Didn't you hear us singing?"

Ginny looked at me, then at Alma. "It's the fever, Josie," she said. "Just rest a while longer. You'll be all right." She glanced at Alma. "Let's have some of that tea you mentioned."

Alma nodded. "I'll get some for all of us."

"Use Granny Ola's pretty cups," Ginny said. "The ones with the pink roses."

"I know where they're at," Sara said, looking right at me.

Ginny sat down on the bed beside me. "You'll like Granny Ola's tea set, Josie."

"Why, because Sara and *my* great-grandmother sipped tea out of them?" Anyway, I wanted to see Ola again, not her tea set. I knew that she must be right outside. Ginny fluffed up the pillows and propped me up. When the tea was ready, Sara hopped up on the foot of the bed. Then Alma brought in the pot and four cups on a tray. She filled a cup for each of us. "I put lots of honey in your cup, Josie. That hyssop will get rid of your sore throat and cough."

I almost spit it out when I first tasted it, but the warm tea did feel good on my throat. I wondered if their tea was the same as mine because Ginny wasn't sipping hers. "I remember how Granny Ola always served tea in these little cups," she said.

"Yes'm, me, too," Sara said, as she put her finger through the handle. She stared at me over her cup and clutched her apple head doll in her other arm. I thought she was trying to irritate me still.

As I slid my finger through the handle, the cup rattled in the saucer. Finally, I steadied it. "The tea is good, Alma, but it makes my lips tingle."

"It's because they're all cracked and dried out, Josie. You'll feel better soon now that your fever broke."

As I studied the pink roses painted on the side of my cup, I saw the stain on the palm of my hand. Stained with huckleberry juice. If I wasn't with Ola, how did the stain get there?

~

The tea made me feel better. About an hour later, Ginny told me I could put on clean clothes and stay up a while. I was still weak, so she helped me into a shirt and jeans. I didn't show her my hand. I wanted to find those huckleberries to see for myself.

"Isn't there a dress I can wear?" I asked.

"A dress?" She felt my forehead. "You've never liked wearing dresses before."

She was right. I must still have a fever.

Ginny walked to the window and stared outside. "I invited a few more friends over today. The eighty-five degree weather is nice. Just right for eating outside."

"Fresh after that rain, too," Alma said. "Been humid." Then she grabbed Sara by the hand. "Come on, Sara. I've got a job for you," Alma said, and they left the room.

Ginny stood at the window looking outside. "Funerals aren't all bad, I guess, Josie. People see folks they haven't seen in years, and we visit and catch up on what we've all been doing and going through." Her voice trailed off. Before she left to join her guests outside, Ginny looked at me and smiled. "You remind me of Granny Ola."

"How?" I asked, grinning.

"Headstrong. Stubborn. Beautiful. A little wild. It's easy to see how families are related in some way."

"Maybe, Mama," I said, feeling closer to her than I ever had before. "Maybe I could try to make a new friend, even if she curls her hair in rags."

Ginny stared at me. "You called me Mama."

"I know."

She kissed me on the forehead and held me real tight. "I'm glad you're trying to be friends with Sara. She's very sweet, and she loved Granny Ola so much. Come on out and join the company if you feel like it."

After Ginny left, I sat there glowing in a new feeling.

Ola and Me

I went over to Granny Ola's dresser. It was filled with perfume bottles, old letters, loose powder, and strings of homemade necklaces hanging from the mirror. I tried on a necklace and admired myself.

Sara came up behind me. "You going through your great-grandmother's things?" She ran her fingers over one of Ola's necklaces and held it up for me to see. "Miss Ola wore this when she went to town."

I wanted to like Sara, but when she said things about Ola I didn't know, it just made me feel more left out. I pulled a curled-up snapshot from in between the mirror and its frame. "Look, Sara, it's my baby picture. We have one like it at home." I turned it over to read what was written on the back.

Dear Granny Ola,

I wish you could see Josephine. She has your eyes, and her little fingers are long and slim like yours, too. Maybe I can drive up there soon.

Love, Ginny

I tried to imagine Granny Ola staring at my baby photo.

"Miss Ola showed it to me already," Sara mumbled. "You were bald as old Bald Knob Hill."

"Is that somewhere around here?"

"It's supposed to be a mountain without nothing growing on top," she muttered.

I grinned and stuck my tongue out at her in a friendly sort of way. Seemed Sara was jealous of me, too. I put the picture back in the mirror frame. The sun had sifted through the windowpane and danced on one of Granny Ola's perfume bottles, throwing a rainbow against the wall. I dusted the small bottle and twisted the top so I could sniff the dried-up perfume. "This is what Ola smelled like. It's the same smell as on her nightgown."

"That's right," Sara piped up. "She wore it all the time."

"You know so much about Ola," I said. I left the top off the perfume bottle.

"You're gonna lose all of the sweet scent from that bottle," Sara replied.

"I want to keep on smelling Granny Ola," I said. "Once we had a puppy. It cried all night, so Ginny put it to bed in the dirty clothes basket. She said that the puppy would calm down and sleep if it could smell us in our underwear and shirts."

"Did it do some good?" Sara asked.

"Yes. I remember I laughed at Ginny's idea, but it worked on the puppy." And on me when I woke up sick yesterday. I felt better when I buried my nose in Ola's clothes.

I put the top back on the perfume bottle and rummaged through the stacks of old letters and photographs.

I found a picture of Ola. Her blue eyes stared at me. Even when I ducked to the side, they still followed.

All of a sudden I felt dizzy, so I hung on to the bedpost. Sara ran out to find her mama. When my eyes straightened up, I could see Ola's dresses hanging from a wire that stretched across the corner of the room. I grabbed a pretty dress with big roses on the front and pulled it over my head. It hung past my feet, so I pulled it up over the sash.

A big straw hat hanging on a nail caught my eye. I took an artificial flower out of a dusty vase and blew on it. I almost sneezed from all the dust clouding around my head. Then I pinned the flower on the rim and pulled the hat over my eyes. I picked up Ola's crooked walking stick, found a bucket propped right by the door, and walked outside.

I leaned on Granny Ola's cane until I felt steady enough to walk. Ola's many friends gawked at me and laughed. Someone said, "Now isn't that the cutest thing. Why, at first, I thought it was Ola."

I didn't want Ginny to see me, and if I could just act natural, nobody would stop me. I took off on the other side of a clump of pine trees, the path that Ola and me came through. Rocky followed me, whining and nipping at my heels. He ran ahead and I followed him. Every so often he stopped to pee. I couldn't see how he could go so much, but every time he sniffed at a tree or bush, he'd raise his hind leg and dribble a bit.

I heard a small voice yell at him. "Git on there, you lazy old hound."

I stopped in my tracks. "Sara! Are you following me?"

"I'm goin' with you."

"What for? You've got on your Sunday dress."

"Someone has to look after you. You've been sick."
She stared at me, determined.

"I don't need your help," I said, lifting Ola's
long dress and following Rocky into the woods. I
didn't care if Sara kept up or not, but I could hear
her right behind me, crunching the leaves under her
feet.

I pushed Ola's crooked cane under a rotten log.
Sure enough, mushrooms poked their tiny umbrella
faces out at me. If Ola was with me, she'd have picked
them right there. But I stumbled past them, and soon
recognized the place where me and Ola had been
before. Ginny had said I was dreaming with the fever,
but I knew I was with Ola.

"I was right here," I shouted, swinging my bucket
around. It slipped from my hands and clattered to the
ground. "This very spot! Ola and me. We picked
berries."

"I know you were here."

I waved my hands in the air. "How'd you know? Did you see Ola, too?"

She glared at me and put her hands on her hips just like Ola did on our walk. "All I know is I came with you. You were delirious and stomped right out of Ola's place."

"Did you come to the church with us, too?" I asked.

"With us? Who's us?"

"Ola and me. We went to the church and sang at the funeral."

"You were in Miss Ola's bed most of the time. You didn't leave and go to the church with her."

I stuck my hands stained with berries out at her. "Explain this!"

Was It a Dream?

Sara sighed and frowned at me. "I gave you some berries out here. You were hot and thirsty, and I stuck 'em in your hand. All you did was squeeze them. I finally got you back to the house. You were a mess. I had to wash you up, or we'd both get in trouble."

"I don't remember that," I said, turning my back on her and walking ahead. "You're making that up."

"I am not!" Sara hollered.

I ignored her and listened to the wind whistling above the trees. I could hear them murmur, like they were talking. Moaning, sort of. I rushed on after Rocky.

"You better wait," Sara said, trying to run ahead of me. "Slow your long legs down, Josie." She stopped to get her breath and shouted, "Stop, I want to show you somethin'." Then she pulled away some vines.

I couldn't believe what I saw. "Sara! You found the willow tree."

She looked at me and poked her lower lip out. "How'd you know about the willow tree? I never showed it to you."

"Ola and me swung on it just a while ago. I told you that. She kept me from flying too high into the air."

"That's my story!" Sara yelled. "Ola done showed *me* how to ride a willow limb, and I told you about it while you was feverish. You only dreamed it."

"It was not a dream," I said through my clenched teeth. "We rode on it like a seesaw." I dropped my basket and Ola's cane and pulled the limb down so Sara could get on it. "Climb on. I'll show you."

Sara pulled her pretty lace dress up around her

waist and threw one white-stockinged leg over the limb. I bunched Ola's dress above my hips and climbed on behind her. "Scoot up some, Sara. I'm about to fall off."

"Shouldn't be doing this in my Sunday dress."

"Well, why'd you wear it today?"

" 'Cause it's Sunday, and we've been to church. You lost a day, remember?"

I didn't feel like I'd lost a day, because Ola and me had been doing things together.

Sara scooted over and we seesawed up and down. Up and down, just like I did with Ola. I could almost hear her laughing.

"I still say you was just dreaming."

"You don't know everything," I shot back.

"I know what I know," Sara said. "You had a fever and was out of your mind. You just don't want to admit it."

Sara hopped down and started toward Granny Ola's place. I went up and down on the limb one more time. Then I slid off and picked up Ola's bucket. I wanted to explore farther into the woods. Rocky sniffed at my heels. Was Sara right? It was along here that Ola and me picked the berries.

"Rocky," I shouted, "would you let me know if a bear was poking around here?"

"He's having so much fun barking all around the bushes, he couldn't hear no bear," Sara yelled from up the hill. "Anyway, I'm tired of watching you. Let's go back."

"Not yet," I hollered. I saw a huckleberry bush, with big, ripe, juicy blue berries. I threw the crooked cane down and ran toward it, ripping those berries off till my hands were dark purple. As I reached out to pick another bunch, something held my hand back. I looked around for Granny Ola. I felt her near me.

Rocky barked at the bush, jumping and growling like he'd treed a coon.

"Scoot, you old hound! Let me in there." But Rocky pushed me away. Then I got worried. "What is it, boy?"

"Come on, Josie," Sara screamed. "Let's go back."

"Go on, scairty cat." I stepped backward and tripped over Ola's cane.

I grabbed the cane, feeling its smooth, worn wood inside my hand. I held it like a baseball bat and sniffed the air. I didn't smell any old stinking bear.

But Rocky yelped and jumped back. Then he took off running up the hill.

"Get back here, Rocky!" I yelled as I kicked the dirt under my feet.

"Come on, Josie," Sara pleaded. "I'm goin'."

"I'm not ready. I want to pick these berries."

"Josie, you're as stubborn as Miss Ola."

I got up off the ground and pushed back the tall grass where Rocky had been barking, and saw something that sent a sharp chill up my back. "Snake!" I yelled. I grabbed the half-full bucket of berries and ran after Rocky and Sara.

Sara and Me

I walked along with my eyes half shut, holding Ola's cane and dragging the bucket of huckleberries. I had to stop several times and pull Ola's dress up over the sash around my waist so I wouldn't trip over the hem. Then I heard something pressing down on a pile of tree limbs. Quietly, I crept ahead and around a curve in the path. Just as I reached a large tree, someone shouted, *"Boo!"*

I screamed and threw my hands up in the air, forgetting all about the bucket of berries. The huckleberries splattered all over the tree and down Sara's lacy Sunday dress.

"Sara!" I yelled. "Why'd you surprise me like that?"

"I was just playing, but you done ruined my Sunday dress."

"I'm sorry. I didn't mean to throw my berries at you."

"Sorry's not good enough," Sara yelled, tears streaming down her face. "My mama's gonna kill me for sure."

"I'm still sorry, Sara," I said, trying to look all serious, but Sara was such a sight I just couldn't keep from laughing. A giggle slipped from my mouth.

"It's not funny," Sara yelled. She poked her lip out, but all at once she started laughing instead.

Rocky sniffed both of us, and licked the huckleberries off Sara's dress. Sara gently pushed me over and tickled my ribs. "You'll be sorry you threw those berries."

"Hey, you jumped out at me, like you were a bear."

We rolled over in the sand, laughing, beating off Rocky's wet licks. I had forgotten all about being sick.

"You're just like Miss Ola," Sara said.

I lay real still, trying to get my breath. "You mean it?"

Sara nodded, staring into my eyes. Then we heard Ginny and Alma calling for us.

We jumped up and brushed the sand from our clothes, but the harder I brushed, the worse I rubbed the berry stain into Sara's dress.

"Ouch," she cried. "Not so hard."

"Sara, I can't get out the stain." She looked at me like she was my mama. "Put Miss Ola's hat back on, Josie, and hush up."

I jammed on Granny Ola's hat and swung her crooked cane. Sara and I held hands and headed home. We saw Zack coming down the rutted road looking for us. "Hey, little ones," he yelled, "your mamas are up in arms and singing a battle song."

"Our mamas needn't of worried about us none. We're doing all right."

"Yes," Sara said, "we're friends now."

We walked back together with Zack, and he slipped

something into my hand. "Ginny told me you might like this, Josie."

I opened my fingers and saw a rock, all dried up and smelling like a faded rose. "The rose rock Ola gave you," I whispered. "You said you'd always keep it, and you did. Thank you!"

I looked up and saw Ginny coming down the path toward us. She ran to me and felt my forehead. "Feel okay, Josie?"

"I'm feeling just fine, Mama."

Sara turned to Ginny and smiled. "Josie acts just like Miss Ola."

I squeezed Sara's hand. I didn't care anymore if she knew Ola better than I did. After all, Ola needed a little girl to keep her company and to drink tea with. I only wished I'd been with them. We both belonged here. Right where Ola had lived. I guess Ola was close to me the same as if I'd been here and gone berry picking with her myself.

"I wish you'd stay here, Josie," Sara said.

"Really?" I asked, feeling proud Sara wanted me up here at Ola's place. "Mama, how long will we be here?"

"Oh, there's so much to do, we'll be here at least another week."

"Could you ever move up here?" Sara asked.

"Move?" Ginny said, a big surprise on her face. "Way up here?"

"Sure," I said. "We could live in Ola's place."

"We have a home, Josie."

"Please, Mama. You could write your card jingles up here just as easy as back home. And it's not like we ever stay anywhere long enough to call it home."

She looked at me with sad eyes. "We'll be here a week or so, taking care of Granny Ola's business. We'll make it a fine time, and you and Sara can play together."

Sara and I grinned at each other and clasped hands. I got excited thinking how we'd explore Ola's woods.

Just then Alma noticed Sara's huckleberry-covered dress. "What in tarnation did you fall into, child?"

I stood there looking gog-eyed, but I was afraid to tell Alma it was my fault. Besides, it wasn't all my fault, what with my addled mind and all. And Sara was the one who jumped out from that tree, making me think she was a bear.

Alma jerked Sara's dress over her head and scrubbed her down with icy well water. Sara stood there screaming her rag-tailed head off. I couldn't help but laugh at the sight, but just as I guffawed real loud, mama grabbed me by the arm and said, "Come on, Josie, you need to rinse yourself off." But she didn't make me undress or get under that cold water. After all, I'd been sick.

~

After supper, Sara and me jumped into Ola's bed and pulled the covers up to our chins. Her cold body made me shiver, so I turned my back to her. That way she could get real close and warm up. We peered over the tops of the quilts, counting all of Ola's dresses hanging on the wire.

We talked all about Ola. "Miss Ola sure knew the names of trees and flowers," Sara said. "She was all the time picking wildflowers and putting jars of them in the house and in the outhouse. That was before she had one inside."

I got so sleepy, Sara's words faded in and out. "What's inside?"

"The toilet," Sara said as she sighed, like she was going to sleep.

"You mean she put flowers inside the toilet?" I asked.

"No, silly. Inside the outhouse shed." She yawned and mumbled, "You're so silly."

I lay there with my eyes closed, and felt myself smiling, thinking how Ola had put wildflowers in her outhouse. She made even the outdoors look homey. Just like her zinnias around her mailbox. She didn't keep her house too clean, but she knew how to grow things and make delicious fried pies. I wouldn't mind having a pie right now. I opened my eyes and stared at her picture. Just looking at her made me feel warm inside. I wondered if she'd ever speak to me again. They all said I was dreaming, but Ola sure seemed real. So real that I feel her with Sara and me, like she's happy that we made friends.

Sure enough, I had gotten to know Granny Ola 'bout as well as I know myself. Didn't Sara tell me I did things same as Ola? I looked out the window at all the trees around the house, especially the pine trees. They grew close together like families, and reached toward the light, as though trying to understand where they belonged, and what they were supposed to do with their lives. Just like mama and me.